WOODS

THE · SPECKS'
· OAK · TREE ·

THE · LITTLES ·
· LIVE · HERE ·

THE LITTLES
to the Rescue

Story and pictures by JOHN PETERSON

Platt & Munk, Publishers/New York
A Division of Grosset & Dunlap

To Elizabeth
who was born
just as I finished
this story

Chapter One

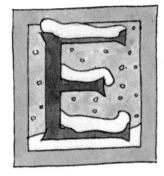verything is ready for the new baby," said Mr. Little to Mrs. Little. "There's nothing for you to worry about."

"Yes there is," said Mrs. Little. She sat next to Mr. Little on their living-room sofa. "Aunt Lily is not here."

"Look!" said Mr. Little. He pointed to Granny Little. "See—Granny has the diapers ready."

Granny Little was sitting in her rocking chair with a pile of diapers in her lap. She held the diapers up and smiled at Mrs. Little. "I cut all of them from one of Mr. Bigg's white handkerchiefs," she said.

"And look, Mother," said ten-year-old Tom Little. "Here's the baby rattle I promised to make. I made it from the smallest peanut shell I could find. And I used part of a toothpick for the handle."

"It's too big," said Tom's younger sister, Lucy.

"I know it's kind of big," said Tom Little. "But I couldn't find anything smaller that would work."

"I hope it's a girl," said Lucy.

Mr. Little laughed. "Why don't we wait and see whether it's a boy or a girl. In a few days we'll know."

"If Aunt Lily doesn't get here soon," said Mrs. Little, "I don't know what I'll do."

"Umph!" snorted Uncle Pete. He banged his cane on the floor. Then he climbed out of his chair and limped over to the fireplace. He added a twig to the fire. "I wish George Bigg would turn up the heat. Doesn't he know that's the first snow of winter out there?"

The Littles were tiny people. Mr. William T. Little, the tallest Little, was only six inches tall. Lucy Little, who was eight years old, was the smallest Little. She was almost four inches tall.

Because the Littles were so tiny, they could live in the walls of George Bigg's house. They lived in ten small rooms that took up only a little space. They always kept out of sight. The Biggs didn't know the Littles were living with them.

THE · LITTLE · FAMILY

MR. LITTLE · MRS. LITTLE · TOM · LUCY

There was one other thing about the Littles that was different from ordinary people. The Littles had tails. There didn't seem to be any reason for the Littles to have tails. They couldn't *do* anything with them. They couldn't hang by their tails. And they didn't wag them when they were happy.

But the Littles liked their tails. They kept them combed and brushed. They tried never to drag their tails on the floor. If a Little was seen dragging his tail, the other Littles knew he was sick with a fever. And he was put right to bed and given a chip from the family's aspirin tablet.

Mrs. Little's tail was nowhere near the floor, but the other Littles were worried about her anyway. Mr. and Mrs. Little's third child was going to be born soon. Aunt Lily Little, the nurse, had helped when Tom and Lucy were born. Mrs. Little wanted her to help this time, too. But Aunt Lily hadn't come yet. The Littles were doing everything they could to keep Mrs. Little from thinking about it.

"Here's the old matchbox cradle," said Mr. Little. "I dragged it out of the closet where it's been since Lucy was a baby."

"Please stop, Will," said Mrs. Little. "I know you are all trying to cheer me up. But I'm not going to feel right until Aunt Lily is here."

"It will stop snowing soon, I'm sure," said Mr. Little. "Then Cousin Dinky will bring her."

"Why can't Cousin Dinky fly when it's snowing?" said Lucy Little. "I thought he put skis on his glider whenever it snowed."

"Golly, Lucy!" said Tom. "You wouldn't want Cousin Dinky to fly in a *storm* with his own mother, would you?"

"Aunt Lily is supposed to help," said Lucy. "It's her job. She's a nurse!"

Lucy Little turned to her mother. "Right, Mother?"

Mrs. Little took her daughter's hand. "Tom is right, dear," she said. "Cousin

GRANNY LITTLE · UNCLE PETE · COUSIN DINKY · AUNT LILY

Dinky shouldn't fly in a snowstorm. That would be too dangerous."

"Why can't Dad and I go get Aunt Lily? We could go on the Biggs' cat," said Tom. "A cat like Hildy could get through that snowstorm."

"Oh dear," said Mrs. Little. "I wish you wouldn't get such ideas, Tom."

"That cat would never go so far away from its home," said Uncle Pete. "Lily lives *four* houses away."

"Hildy will do anything I tell her to," said Tom.

"I still don't see why Cousin Dinky doesn't fly right through the snowstorm," said Lucy. "He's a wonderful pilot. He's brave as anything. And there isn't a thing he can't do."

"Your Cousin Dinky might fly in a storm if he were by himself," said Mr. Little. "He is an adventurer, after all. But he would never take a chance like that with his mother along."

"Are you sure?" said Mrs. Little. "I wish Aunt Lily were here, but I don't want them to take any chances."

"It would be very foolish of them to try it," said Mr. Little. "That's a bad storm out there. I almost got blown off the roof."

"Why don't you phone and tell them not to come?" said Mrs. Little. "I'd feel better if I knew for sure they weren't coming. Oh dear, what am I saying? I want Aunt Lily here more than I've wanted anything."

"You'd better make that phone call, Will," said Uncle Pete. "Dinky has good sense. But that mother of his—umph! She may talk him into it. If she decides we need her over here, she'll come—snowstorm or not."

"I'll call tonight," said Mr. Little. "We can use the Emergency Telephone Plan. Cousin Dinky and Aunt Lily will be waiting by the phone at the usual time. Tom, you can come with me. I'll need your help to lift the receiver off the hook."

Chapter Two

Meanwhile Aunt Lily was doing some reading. She was in the attic of a house owned by Dr. Dan Zigger, four houses away from the Littles.

Aunt Lily and her son Dinky kept on living in the walls of the Zigger house after Dinky's father died. The Littles wanted them to come and live in the Biggs' house, but Aunt Lily wouldn't do it. She didn't want to get too far away from Dr. Zigger's house.

Dr. Zigger's office was in his home. Aunt Lily had learned how to be a nurse by reading the old medical books Dr. Zigger kept in the attic. And she learned a lot by watching Dr. Zigger take care of his patients. If she were living with the Littles, she wouldn't be able to read the books or to watch Dr. Zigger. What kind of a nurse would she be then?

Today Aunt Lily was reading her favorite book about babies for the third time. The big book was open on the attic floor. Aunt Lily stood above the book on a shoe box filled with old photographs. She turned the pages by using the eraser end of a pencil.

Before Aunt Lily invented that way of turning pages, she had to climb down from the shoe box every time she wanted to turn a page.

In the middle of an interesting chapter on vitamins, Aunt Lily suddenly remembered something. She had not yet packed her nurse's bag with supplies.

"My stars!" she said. "I'm surprised at myself. If I ever showed up at the Littles without the right supplies, I'd be ashamed to death."

Aunt Lily climbed down from the shoe box. She walked to the small attic window and climbed up on the windowsill. Snowflakes were falling against the glass. "This is terrible," she said. "Why doesn't it stop snowing? They need me at the Littles, and here I am snowbound—helpless!"

The tiny nurse took a deep breath. "Calm yourself, Lily," she said. She looked through the window to the white trees beyond the yard. Then she smiled. "If the snow weren't so beautiful," said Aunt Lily, "I'd hate it. But I don't, and that's that."

Aunt Lily turned and hurried off to look for her nurse's bag.

Suddenly she stopped and put a finger to her head. "There's something else I must remember. What is it?" Aunt Lily thought for a moment. "Oh yes!" she said. "Dinky and I must be at the telephone at three o'clock in the morning. If the Littles need me, they will call. And snowstorm or no snowstorm, I'll go!"

Chapter Three

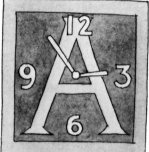

t five minutes before three o'clock the next morning, the snow was still coming down hard. Mr. Little and Tom Little climbed up the telephone cord to the table in the hall of the Biggs' house. Each Little was carrying a big wad of cotton.

"Now stuff the cotton under the telephone at this end," said Mr. Little. "That's where the bell is. The cotton will keep the phone from ringing loud."

"Who's going to call us?" said Tom. "I thought we were going to call Aunt Lily and Cousin Dinky."

"We are," said Mr. Little. "But we should stuff the bell just in case we get a call first."

"Aren't we only supposed to make calls if there's an emergency?" said Tom.

"That's the plan, yes," said Mr. Little. "But we're going to call Aunt Lily anyway. You know her. She might try anything, and we don't want her to come out in the snowstorm."

"I like her," said Tom. "She's terrific."

"Let's get the receiver off the hook," said Mr. Little.

The tiny man and his son pushed the heavy telephone receiver off the hook. It rested on the telephone above the dial.

The dial tone buzzed.

"You stand on one of the buttons, Tom," said Mr. Little.

Tom got onto the telephone and did as his father told him. The receiver stopped buzzing. "Now we wait for the Biggs' grandfather clock to strike three," said Mr. Little. "As soon as it does, you hop off the button and I'll dial Dr. Dan Zigger's number."

"What should I do if someone calls before that?" said Tom.

"Just hop off the button as fast as you can," said Mr. Little. "We don't want the ringing to wake up any of the Biggs."

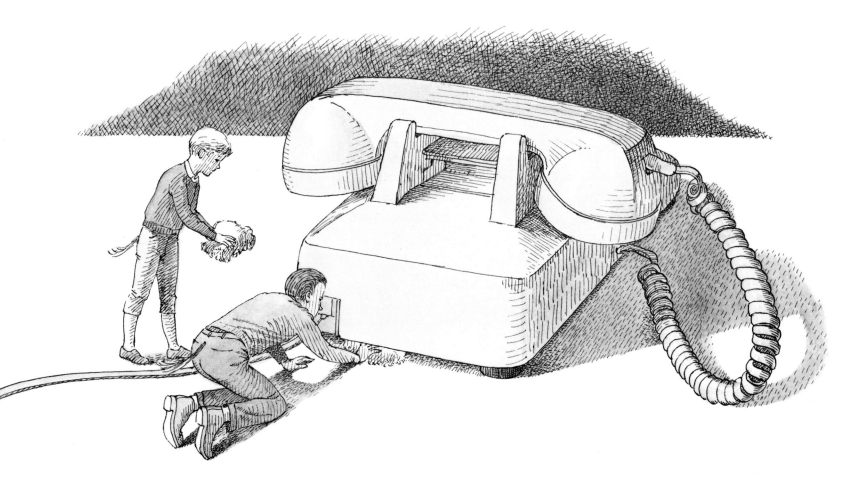

At the same time Aunt Lily and Cousin Dinky were waiting by the telephone at Dr. Dan Zigger's house. They had stuffed cotton under the bell of Dr. Zigger's telephone. The receiver was off the hook. Cousin Dinky was standing on one of the cut-off buttons. And Aunt Lily was standing by the receiver.

"I'm sure they'll call," said Aunt Lily. "I feel it in my bones that the baby is on the way."

"It's still snowing like mad," said Cousin Dinky. "You don't expect me to take you to Uncle Will's in this storm, do you?"

"If they call, I certainly do," said Aunt Lily. "I was there when Tom was born, and I was there when Lucy was born. You might as well make up your mind—I'm going to be there when this baby is born."

"Mother," said Cousin Dinky, "we can't—"

"You can fly in storms," said Aunt Lily. "You've flown in storms before."

"That's different—I was alone."

"I don't see the difference," said Aunt Lily. "If *you* can fly in a storm, *we* can fly in this storm if we have to. And that is that."

"Not in my glider you won't," said Cousin Dinky. "I'm not getting you killed."

"Now listen, Dinky dear," said Aunt Lily. "*If* the Littles call, it means they need me. And I'm going to be there to help, one way or the other. Either you fly me there or I *walk*. I go where I'm needed. And that's that."

"You couldn't walk there, Mother," said Cousin Dinky. "It's a two-day trip in good weather."

"I'll go."

"Wow!" said Cousin Dinky. "You really mean it, don't you?"

The phone rang.

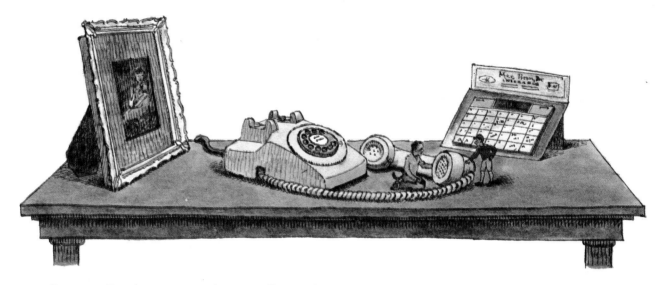

Cousin Dinky was so busy talking, he forgot to hop off the button and answer the telephone. When he finally remembered, the telephone had already rung for a few seconds.

"Oh-oh," said Cousin Dinky. "I hope that didn't wake anybody up."

"Hello ... hello." It was Mr. Little's voice coming from the receiver. "Cousin Dinky? Aunt Lily? Who's there?"

Just then a light was turned on in the Ziggers' bedroom. Aunt Lily and Cousin Dinky could hear voices.

Cousin Dinky jumped off the phone and stood by the receiver. "Hello, Uncle Will ... this is Dinky," he whispered.

"Dinky ... hello ... how are you?" said Mr. Little.

Suddenly the door to the bedroom opened. Dr. Zigger came out. He was putting on his bathrobe. He walked toward the telephone, yawning.

Aunt Lily and Cousin Dinky moved quickly. They slid down the telephone cord to the floor. They then hid under the table and listened.

"What's this?" said Dr. Zigger. "The phone is off the hook." He picked up the receiver. "Anybody there? ... What's that? ... A baby? Who's having a baby?"

The doctor waited a moment. "No, this is not your Cousin Dinky. You must have the wrong number. I'm—well I'll be ..." He hung up.

"What is it, dear?" It was Mrs. Zigger calling from the bedroom. "Anything wrong?"

"Someone's having a baby, I think," said Dr. Zigger. "But I don't think it was for me ... wrong number." He hung up the receiver. "Strange." The doctor scratched his chin. "Oh well, if it's for me, they'll call back."

Dr. Dan Zigger walked toward the bedroom. He stopped and looked back. "The phone was off the hook. How did the call come through? That's odd. Ellen? Did you have the phone off the hook for some reason?"

No answer.

"Boy! I wish I could fall asleep like that. She must not have a worry in the world." Dr. Zigger closed the bedroom door and turned off the light.

Aunt Lily grabbed Cousin Dinky by the arm. "The baby is coming!" she said. "We've got to go. I *must* be there. The Littles need me, or they wouldn't have called. You will be a dear, won't you, Dinky, and take me?"

"I can hardly believe it," said Cousin Dinky. "They want us to fly in this storm."

"It's an emergency," said Aunt Lily. "Something must be wrong. If it weren't an emergency, they wouldn't have called. They need a nurse."

"I suppose you're right," said Cousin Dinky. "Let's get your things into the glider. We'll take off at dawn. With luck, the storm may be over by then."

"That may be too late," said Aunt Lily. "We should leave *now*."

"Oh, Mother!" said Cousin Dinky. "Do you know what you're asking me to do? I've never flown at night in my life!"

Chapter Four

It was still dark when Cousin Dinky got ready to fly Aunt Lily to the Littles. And the snow was still falling.

Cousin Dinky always flew from roof-top to roof-top on his glider flights. For one thing, there was less chance of meeting up with big people that way. And it was easy for Cousin Dinky to take off in his glider from a roof. He would let the light glider coast down the roof until it picked up enough speed to fly.

Once in the air, Cousin Dinky always tried to fly with the wind. That was the easiest and fastest way. In a storm, however, the wind sometimes blew every which way.

Cousin Dinky was an expert pilot. For the last few years he had flown up and down the Big Valley visiting tiny people. He went wherever the wind took him.

Tonight he knew he was going to need to remember everything he had learned on those flights. And tonight Cousin Dinky was scared.

For all his adventuring ways, the tiny pilot did not like to take chances. He was an adventurer, not a dare-devil. And when he had to take a chance and risk getting hurt, he wanted to do it alone.

But Cousin Dinky knew he couldn't make this flight alone, and that was what scared him. The Littles didn't need him—they needed his mother. And he was the only person who could get her there on time. Suddenly Cousin Dinky wished with all his heart that he wasn't a glider pilot.

"That's silly!" said Cousin Dinky aloud. "I am, and that's all there is to it."

"What's silly?" said Aunt Lily.

"Nothing, Mother," said Cousin Dinky. "Here, let me help you with that parachute harness." He checked over the straps on Aunt Lily's parachute.

When Aunt Lily and Cousin Dinky got out on the roof, the wind was blowing hard. It blew the snow wildly about them. The glider was tied near the chimney. The heat from the chimney usually kept the snow from piling up and covering the glider.

"We're going to have to make some kind of runway," said Cousin Dinky. "The snow is too deep. The glider's skis will sink into the snow, and we won't be able to get up enough speed to take off."

Cousin Dinky made a ball of snow and rolled it along the top of the roof. He rolled it until it got to be the size of a snowball. Then he rolled it in front of the glider and gave the snowball a big push down the roof.

The snowball moved slowly at first. The bigger it grew, the faster it went. When the snowball finally fell over the edge of the roof, it left a path—a runway for the glider.

The two tiny people climbed into the glider. Aunt Lily sat behind Cousin Dinky. "Fasten your seat belt, Mother," Cousin Dinky yelled. "This is going to be a rough ride."

Cousin Dinky pulled in the fish-hook anchor that was holding the glider to the roof. The glider began to slide down the steep slope of the roof. It moved fast on the slippery runway. Just as the glider got to the edge of the roof, Cousin Dinky raised the wing flaps. The glider rose into the air. It zoomed out over the Ziggers' yard.

Cousin Dinky was surprised. It was very dark, but the darkness didn't seem to bother him. Then he knew that much of his flying was done by *feeling* his way through the air. Cousin Dinky tried to find winds that would carry his glider higher.

Aunt Lily was not a flier. She was busy looking at the lights of the houses below. The falling snow made the lights look fuzzy. They looked as if they had halos around them. "Oh, Dinky!" said Aunt Lily. "I've never seen anything so beautiful."

Cousin Dinky flew the glider in a wide circle, riding the wind higher and higher. Finally, when they were above the trees, the tiny pilot headed his ship in the direction of the Biggs' house. He thought he could see the dim hall light Mr. Bigg kept on all night, but he wasn't sure.

The wind tossed the glider around like a leaf. Cousin Dinky tried to hold his glider steady. He needed all his strength. But the glider twisted and turned, rose and fell, with the wind.

Somehow Cousin Dinky kept from crashing. "This is stupid!" he shouted. "I'll never fly in a storm again. Not for *anyone*, I won't."

The wind tossed the glider over the dark woods. Black trees reached up like giant hands. Suddenly the little ship was caught in a powerful gust of wind. The glider tipped way over. It was all Cousin Dinky could do to stop it from turning upside down.

A moment later, the Biggs' roof was right in front of Cousin Dinky. He pulled a lever. Two parachutes came open with a crack. The parachutes were fixed to the glider's body. They acted like a brake, slowing the ship. The glider skidded into the soft snow on the roof.

Cousin Dinky jumped from the cockpit and pulled in the parachutes before they could drag the glider off the roof. Then he hooked the fish-hook anchor to the chimney and tied the glider down.

"We made it, Mother!" he yelled. "We made it!" Cousin Dinky hopped up on the glider's wing to help Aunt Lily down.

Her seat was empty.

Chapter Five

The snowstorm stopped at daybreak. But before then Cousin Dinky flew his glider into the storm three times more, looking for his mother. He went back and forth between the Biggs' house and Dr. Zigger's house, trying to see through the darkness to the ground. Finally, just before daybreak, he spotted a parachute in the woods between the two houses.

When Cousin Dinky got back to the Biggs' house he told the Littles what had happened. They all sat down at the dining-room table to talk over what should be done.

Mrs. Little served hot cocoa that Mr. Little had taken from the Biggs. The Littles got everything they needed from the Biggs when the Biggs weren't looking. The cocoa was left over from the Biggs' supper.

Cousin Dinky sat with his head in his hands. Uncle Pete patted him on the shoulder. "We'll get her out of those woods, Dinky," he said. "I can promise you that."

"Why doesn't the boy drink his cocoa?" said Granny Little. "He needs it for energy."

"At least we know where Aunt Lily landed," said Mr. Little. "And that she opened her parachute. It could be worse, Dinky."

The glider pilot kept his head in his hands. "If only I could have landed. But the trees were too thick. I'm surprised her parachute didn't get caught in the branches."

Cousin Dinky went on, "She's been in that storm since four o'clock. And we don't even know if she landed without getting hurt. Have you any idea how fast that wind was blowing?"

"It was terrible," said Mr. Little. "And I feel bad that our telephone message got mixed up, and you thought Aunt Lily was needed right away."

"We shouldn't have called," said Uncle Pete. "It wasn't an emergency."

"Dinky, you should get some rest," said Granny Little. "Flying that glider back and forth until the sun came up—you must be dead tired."

"I *had* to find her," said Cousin Dinky.

"You did the right thing, Cousin Dinky," said Mrs. Little.

"Did she land near the Specks?" said Tom Little. The Specks made their home in a tree in the woods. They were Wood Tinies.

"The parachute is southeast of their oak tree," said Cousin Dinky. "The woods there are deeper."

"I think we should head for Stubby Speck's tree anyway," said Mr. Little. "He may be able to help us."

"Speck stays pretty close to that tree of his in the winter," said Uncle Pete.

"I'm sure he does," said Mr. Little. "But he's bound to know more about the woods than we do."

"I hate to ask you all to help me," said Cousin Dinky. "Mother may already be . . . well, it might be a wild-goose chase."

"She's all right!" said Lucy Little. "Aunt Lily is all right! I *know* she's all right!"

"We may face great danger going after her," said Cousin Dinky. "I . . ."

Uncle Pete held up his hand. "You're not *asking* us to help, Dinky," he said. "We're *helping!* You're part of our family!"

All the Littles nodded.

"I love you, Cousin Dinky," said Lucy Little. She ran to Cousin Dinky and kissed him.

"We all love you, Dinky," said Granny Little.

Uncle Pete banged his cane on the floor and climbed to his feet. "Come on! Let's get Lily out of those dumb woods and back where she belongs."

"I'll find Hildy," said Tom. He ran to the door.

"Hold it, boy!" said Uncle Pete. "We don't need that cat. She'll only give us trouble."

"No she won't, Uncle Pete," said Tom. "Golly! Hildy will do anything I tell her."

"I'm afraid we do need the cat, Uncle Pete," said Mr. Little. "The snow is too deep to walk in. Even with snowshoes, it would be hard going in the woods."

"I agree," said Cousin Dinky. "We'll get there much faster riding on the cat. And time is important. We have to hurry."

Tom Little ran to find the cat.

Mr. Little turned to Uncle Pete. "I think you'd better stay here, Uncle Pete, and look after the women."

"WHAT!" roared Uncle Pete. He stood up and pounded his fist on the table. "You want *me* to stay here with the women?"

Mr. Little looked at Mrs. Little. "I don't mean stay *with* them, Uncle Pete," he said. "I mean stay and take care of them."

"Oh well, that's different," said Uncle Pete. "But you'll need my experience where the greatest danger is." He shrugged his shoulders. "Let Tom stay. It will be good training for him."

"I thought the cat would listen only to Tom," said Cousin Dinky.

"I'll tell that cat what to do," said Uncle Pete. "After all, it's just a house pet."

"I think you should *all* go," said Granny Little. "The Little women can take care of themselves."

"Oh dear," said Mrs. Little. "Do you think so?"

"I'm not afraid," said Lucy Little.

"I wish Aunt Lily were here," said Mrs. Little. She nodded her head. "I really do. I'm very worried about her."

"Why don't you men get going?" said Granny Little. "We'll need Lily here soon."

Chapter Six

Tom Little found Hildy the cat in Henry Bigg's room. Henry was Mr. and Mrs. Bigg's son. He was about Tom's age. Tom liked many of the things Henry liked.

Henry and his friends often played astronaut. Tom loved to watch them. And whenever the Littles visited another tiny family (which wasn't often), Tom and his friends played astronaut, too.

Tom and Lucy Little had known Henry Bigg all their lives. He was very important to them. They thought of him as a friend. The two Little children had spent many happy hours watching Henry and his friends. They would have watched more, but their father said too much watching wasn't good for them.

Henry, of course, didn't know the Little children were alive. It was a rule of the Littles that they would never let the big people know they were living with them. The Little family liked the Bigg family, but they didn't trust them. They didn't know what the Biggs would do if they found out that there were tiny people living in their house.

All the tiny people in the Big Valley felt the same way. They didn't want to take chances. So, Tom and Lucy never tried to talk to Henry Bigg.

When Tom found Hildy in Henry's room, he saw there was going to be trouble. Henry was playing with the cat, as he often did before breakfast. He was lying on his bed with Hildy on his stomach. The cat was batting at a small ball tied to a paddle that Henry held over his chest.

"Golly!" said Tom to himself. "We need that cat, and there she is playing games."

Tom usually whistled a secret whistle when he wanted Hildy to come to him. Most cats won't come when they are called unless they are hungry. Hildy was like that, too. Most of the time she didn't pay attention to Henry when he called her. She would listen to Tom, though. Why she did was a mystery. "Maybe," Mr. Little had once said, "it is because Tom was the first to tame her, and he needs her for important things—not just to play with."

This time Tom didn't dare use the secret whistle to call Hildy. Henry might hear it. Tom would have to get the cat's attention in another way. But how?

Then Tom saw Henry's parakeet. It was in a cage near the window in Henry's room.

"If I let the parakeet out of the cage," thought Tom, "Henry will jump up to catch it. While he's busy, I'll call Hildy."

Poor Tom Little. He forgot how cats feel about birds. Tom climbed up to where the parakeet's cage was hanging. He pulled out a small stick that held the cage door shut. As soon as the door opened, the bird flew out.

Henry saw the parakeet fly over his head. He jumped to his feet and began to chase the bird around the room.

The cat stood on Henry's bed and looked wildly about her. Tom ran from the windowsill to the bed and leaped onto the cat's neck. "To the cellar, Hildy!" Tom commanded.

Then Hildy saw the bird. She leaped up into the air. Tom dug his hands into Hildy's fur and held on with all his might. In one great cat-leap, Hildy went from the bed to the top of Henry's dresser—halfway across the room. Her eyes glittered.

The green and yellow bird flew around Henry's room. It bumped into the walls and the window, trying to find a way out.

Henry climbed over furniture, grabbing at the parakeet. Hildy leaped from the dresser to the bed to Henry's desk and back to the bed. Tom closed his eyes and held on. He was beginning to feel seasick from the ride.

Finally Henry saw that Hildy was chasing the bird, too. "Ma! Ma!" he shouted. "Get Hildy out of here! I'm trying to get the bird back in its cage."

Mrs. Bigg came running. For a moment Tom didn't know what to do. He couldn't jump off Hildy's neck without being killed (at least that is what he thought). But if he stayed there, Mrs. Bigg would see him.

Tom decided to try to hide from Mrs. Bigg without getting off the cat. Hand over hand, the tiny boy moved around the cat's neck until he was underneath it. He needed all his strength. Tom ached all over. His arms were tired. He knew he couldn't hang on much longer. "Oh please, Mrs. Bigg," he whispered. "Help me!"

Finally, just as Tom could stand it no longer, Mrs. Bigg grabbed the cat. She walked quickly with her to the cellar door.

Slam! Click! It was cool and dark. Hildy and Tom were alone in the cellar. It was just where Tom wanted to take Hildy in the first place.

Chapter Seven

hen Aunt Lily fell out of Cousin Dinky's glider, the first thing she thought was, "I'm going to get killed because I didn't fasten my seat belt."

The second thing she thought was, "Now who's going to help the Littles with their new baby?"

Then she remembered her parachute.

The parachute opened with a crack, stopping Aunt Lily's headlong fall. "Ouch!" she said. "That hurt!" But when Aunt Lily looked up and saw the parachute, she felt wonderful. "I'm not going to be killed after all," she said.

The wind blew hard, tossing the tiny woman over the trees. "How do I make this thing land?" she asked herself. Aunt Lily began pulling on the lines of the parachute, trying to make it fall toward the ground.

Aunt Lily was lucky. Without knowing it, she was doing the right thing. When she pulled on the lines, some of the air was forced out from under the parachute. This made it fall faster toward the ground.

The snow was blowing all about Aunt Lily. She didn't even see the trees that almost caught her parachute. But when she looked down, she did see the ground rushing up to meet her. Aunt Lily screamed, closed her eyes, and put her hands over her face.

Once again Aunt Lily was lucky. When she dropped the parachute lines to cover her face, the air filled the parachute again, slowing it down. Aunt Lily fell into a thornbush. Her clothing was torn, but she was not hurt.

Aunt Lily's parachute was stuck in the thornbush. She couldn't touch the ground. She pulled and tugged at the lines, trying to escape.

"What am I doing this for?" Aunt Lily said to herself. "I have scissors in my nurse's bag."

Nurse Lily Little reached in her bag for her scissors and cut the parachute lines. She fell through the thornbush and landed in the snow.

When Aunt Lily sat in the snow under the thornbush, she felt a strange thing. "That's odd," she said. "This snow feels warm. Ridiculous! Whoever heard of warm snow?"

Aunt Lily sniffed. "I smell smoke! Am I on fire?" She jumped up. Then she looked down to where she had been sitting. "My stars!" said Aunt Lily. "It's a chimney!"

Aunt Lily had fallen on some kind of chimney. It came right out of the ground. She wondered what such a thing was doing in the middle of the woods. Someplace, under the ground, somebody had a fire. Aunt Lily tried to see down the chimney hole, but she couldn't see anything. As she leaned over, some more snow fell into the hole.

"Hello!" she yelled down the chimney. "Anybody there? Can you hear me?"

"Oh well, at least I won't freeze to death," thought Aunt Lily. She held her hands in the warm smoke and rubbed them together. "If only Dinky were here. He'd know what to do."

Just then Aunt Lily had a feeling she was being watched. She looked into the darkness. "Who is it?" she whispered.

A shadow moved. She heard a noise behind her. She spun around. Another shadow moved. "Who are you?" said Aunt Lily. Suddenly three figures jumped at her. Aunt Lily screamed. She felt a bag being thrown over her head. Someone stuffed her into it.

"We got one!" said a husky voice. "We got us a Tree Tiny!"

Chapter Eight

t was still early morning when the Littles set out to find Aunt Lily. The yard, the trees, and the woods were covered with snow.

All the Little men were aboard Hildy the cat. First there was Tom, who was high up on the cat's neck. He sent Hildy toward the woods, talking and pulling gently on her ears. This was the boy's way of steering the cat. Hildy moved slowly, lifting her paws high and staying away from the deepest snow drifts.

Behind Tom, on the cat's back, was Cousin Dinky. He looked over Tom's head at the woods. This was the kind of adventure Cousin Dinky would have enjoyed if his mother weren't in danger.

Mr. Little sat behind Cousin Dinky. He was looking at a map. Uncle Pete was last. He was covered from head to foot with a long, heavy coat, and he was armed for battle. He carried a bow and arrows, a needle sword and a spear.

All the Littles were armed. Mr. Little carried a needle sword. Cousin Dinky had a bow and arrows. And Tom carried a red firecracker that had once belonged to Henry Bigg. Each Little was also carrying a wooden match and a birthday candle stuck in his belt.

Mr. Little looked up from his map reading. "There it is, Tom," he said. "There's the path."

Mr. Little pointed to an opening in the woods between two trees. The snow was so deep that it was hard to tell the path from the rest of the ground.

"Keep your eyes open for tracks of wild animals," said Uncle Pete. He looked behind him. "Maybe I should face the rear, in case we're followed."

"It's more important to stay away from dogs," said Mr. Little.

"I wish this cat would move a little faster," said Cousin Dinky.

"You can't hurry a cat," said Uncle Pete. "If they feel like it, they can be as slow as molasses in January."

The Littles were headed for Stubby Speck's oak tree deep in the woods. The Speck family lived in the oldest and largest tree. The Specks became friends of the Littles the summer before, when the Littles were accidentally lost in the woods.

Many years ago Mr. Speck's great-great-grandfather had dug out eight snug rooms in the lowest branch of the tree. He was a very strong tiny person who liked hard work. All the Specks were strong like him. They all worked hard.

The Specks were much more independent than the Littles. The Littles, like most tiny people, needed to take things from the big people with whom they lived. In return, the Littles did work for the Biggs. They looked after the electric wires and the water pipes inside the walls of the house. The Littles kept the wires and pipes in good repair, but the Biggs never knew it.

The Specks had no one from whom to take things. They did everything for themselves. So they spent most of their time during the spring and summer getting ready for winter.

The Specks did this hard work gladly. They didn't want to live with big people, and they couldn't understand why the Littles did.

For half an hour Hildy the cat moved through the snow. She seemed to know where the path was without much help from Tom.

"There it is," said Tom, "the Specks' tree. It sure does look different in the winter."

"Feels different, too," said Uncle Pete. He shivered under his heavy coat.

"How do we get up to their rooms?" said Cousin Dinky. This was his first visit to the Specks.

"We climb up the steps that go around and around the tree trunk," said Mr. Little. "They're so well hidden you can't see them until you get to the bottom of the tree."

The Littles climbed down from Hildy's back onto a root of the tree that was above the snow. Tom turned to Hildy. "Stay, Hildy!" he said. "Stay!"

"We'll have to hurry," said Mr. Little. "The cat won't want to wait in the snow for too long."

The four Littles climbed the long stairway up the tree to the Specks' door. The door, like the steps, was hard to see until they got close to it.

A small string came through a hole next to the door. Mr. Little pulled the string. A bell tinkled inside the tree. The door opened a moment later, and Stubby Speck stood before them.

Chapter Nine

oodness me and a cup of tea!" said Stubby Speck. "We're being invaded by House Tinies. It's the Littles come to visit." The tiny round man shook each Little's hand and pulled him into the room. "What a wonderful surprise!"

Mr. Little introduced Cousin Dinky to Mr. Speck. "Wonderful, wonderful! So you're the famous glider-pilot cousin! Welcome to our home," said Stubby Speck. "Mrs. Speck!" he called. "The House Tinies have come to visit."

Mrs. Speck came into the room followed by her two daughters, Annie and Janie. The girls took Tom into the kitchen to give him a cup of hot sassafras tea.

"We're just finishing breakfast," said Mrs. Speck. "I'll set four more places and you can join us." She started out of the room.

"Just a moment, please, Mrs. Speck," said Mr. Little. "I'm afraid we can't stay. This is not a happy visit, I'm sorry to say. We are in the woods looking for Cousin Dinky's mother."

Mr. Little explained how Aunt Lily had fallen out of the glider and landed in the woods. "And now, here we are. We are hoping you people can tell us something about the part of the woods where Aunt Lily landed."

Mr. Speck looked down at the floor. "Your Aunt Lily may be in even more trouble than you think," he said.

"How's that?" said Uncle Pete.

"I'm sorry, son," said Mr. Speck to Cousin Dinky. "But if your mother is still alive, she may have been captured by the Ground Tinies."

"Ground Tinies?" said Uncle Pete and Cousin Dinky at the same time.

"What are Ground Tinies?" said Mr. Little. "Are they dangerous?"

"We think Ground Tinies are tiny people much like ourselves," said Stubby Speck. "We think they live in underground homes. And—I'm sorry to say it—we think they may be dangerous."

"You say you 'think' these things about Ground Tinies," said Cousin Dinky. "Don't you *know*?"

THE · SPECK · FAMILY

"A few Wood Tinies have disappeared while out hunting in that part of the woods," said Stubby Speck.

"No one has ever seen a Ground Tiny up close," said Mrs. Speck. "Mr. Speck has tried to talk to some."

"They're a sneaky bunch," said Mr. Speck. "Whenever I get near, they run off like scared rabbits."

"That doesn't sound as though they're dangerous," said Mr. Little. "Maybe they're just timid."

Uncle Pete put his hand on his sword handle. "I say we'd better get ready for a fight if we want Lily back."

Meanwhile, in the kitchen, Tom was drinking his second cup of sassafras tea.

"How did you get here through the snow?" said Annie Speck. She sat down beside Tom. Annie was a year older than Tom, and she liked him.

Tom moved his chair away. "We came on a cat," he said.

Janie Speck jumped to her feet. "Oh, let's see her! Where is she?"

"Waiting at the foot of the tree," said Tom.

Janie ran to a round window (it was made from the bottom of a glass bottle) and turned a crank. The bark shutters on the outside of the tree opened and they could see Hildy.

"She's beautiful!" said Janie.

"She's a little fat, isn't she?" said Annie.

"No!" said Tom. "Do you think so?"

"Someone's coming!" said Janie.

"Oh-oh," said Tom. "It's two kids with a *dog.*" He ran to tell the others.

The Littles and the Specks tried to see out the window at the same time. There wasn't enough room for everyone.

Mr. Little stepped back and gave a pushing child his place. "What's happening?" he said.

"That cat is still there," said Stubby Speck. "She hasn't seen the dog."

"The dog hasn't seen the cat, either," said Tom Little.

"I can't see *anything!*" said Janie Speck.

"That dog is sniffing all over the place," said Uncle Pete.

Mrs. Speck stepped away from the window. "Would you like to see, Mr. Little?" she said.

"No thank you, Mrs. Speck," said Mr. Little. "I don't think I could stand to watch. If Hildy runs away and leaves us, I don't know what we'll do."

Suddenly there was a gasp from the watchers at the window. "There she goes!" yelled Mr. Speck. They all left the window and ran to the other side of the room to look out the window on that side of the tree.

"Where's the dog?"

"I can't see Hildy!"

"There she is!"

"Where?"

"Watch out!"

"Look at her run," said Tom. "She sure can run." He was proud.

The tiny people left the window one by one.

"Oh, that poor cat," said Janie Speck.

"What will the dog do to her if he catches her?" said Annie Speck.

"I don't believe a full-grown cat has been caught by a dog since the world began," said Cousin Dinky.

"Then why do they chase them?" said Annie.

"How do we go on with our search without Hildy?" said Mr. Little.

"I knew that cat would let us down," said Uncle Pete. He banged his cane on the oak floor. "I knew it!"

"I hope it's not too late," said Stubby Speck. He put on his hat and coat.

"Where are you going, Mr. Speck?" said Mrs. Speck.

"I'm going to wake up old Skunk," said Mr. Speck, "if he hasn't gone into hibernation. It's only the first snow of winter. He might still be awake."

"Old Skunk?" said Cousin Dinky.

"Mr. Speck has a tame skunk," said Mr. Little. "A wonderful animal! He moves slowly, but no one ever tries to stop him."

"Are you going with us, Speck?" said Uncle Pete.

"I sure am," said Stubby Speck. "You're going into a dangerous and unknown part of the woods. You could never make it on foot, and there's no time to wait for your cat to come back."

Stubby Speck turned to his wife. "Mrs. Speck," he said. "While I'm checking on old Skunk, give these folks some hot biscuits and strawberry jam. They'll need some of your good cooking where they're going."

Chapter Ten

The Littles and their friend Stubby Speck rode the skunk southeast to the wildest part of the woods. The skunk took his time. He picked his way carefully through the deep snow. He moved even slower than Hildy the cat.

"I like your skunk, Mr. Speck," said Cousin Dinky. "But I sure wish he could go a little faster."

"Skunk is in no hurry, *ever*," said Stubby Speck. "I suppose it's because he isn't afraid of any animal in the woods, big or little. I've tried everything to get him to move faster."

"He's a fine animal," said Uncle Pete, "with a mind of his own. 'Slow and steady wins the race' I always say."

"We're just lucky he hadn't gone into his deep winter sleep," said Mr. Little.

The woods grew thicker. Bare bushes looked like huge spider-monsters, guarding the way. There were more trees. Overhead branches grew every which way in jagged black lines. The sky was gray.

"Ground Tinies live in scary places," said Tom Little. "It's spooky around here." Tom moved closer to Uncle Pete.

"Don't get too close, Tom," said Uncle Pete. "I need to have my throwing arm free in case we get ambushed." He held his spear ready.

"Anybody that ambushes this skunk is in for a terrible time," said Stubby Speck.

Cousin Dinky was looking for Aunt Lily's parachute. "If we can only find her parachute," he said, "we may find her nearby."

"This is Ground Tiny country," said Stubby Speck. "I'd be surprised if they haven't captured her already."

"There it is!" said Cousin Dinky. "There's the parachute. It's on that thornbush."

"But where is Lily?" said Uncle Pete.

"We'd better get off Skunk," said Stubby Speck, "and get under that bush for a look around." The woodsman said something in the skunk's ear, and the animal lowered its head. One by one, everyone slid down the skunk's neck to the ground.

Cousin Dinky got to the parachute first. "Nothing," he said. "She's not here. There's not even a footprint."

"The snow covered any footprints," said Stubby Speck.

"She couldn't just disappear into thin air," Cousin Dinky said.

"Hey, Dad! Uncle Pete! Everyone!" It was Tom. "Look at this! Is it a chimney?" The boy had found the chimney where Aunt Lily had landed.

"A Ground Tiny chimney!" said Stubby Speck. "Now we're getting someplace."

He cleared away the snow to get a better look. "Hard to see. How did you find it, son?"

"I felt something warm," said Tom Little. "And there it was."

"That's a chimney?" said Uncle Pete. "Looks like a hollow root to me." He touched it. "Why, it *is* warm."

Mr. Little looked up at a maple tree. "They probably made the chimney from a root of this tree."

"These Ground Tinies are nobody's fools," said Uncle Pete. He looked around, his hand on his sword.

"What do we do now?" said Mr. Little. "The entrance to their underground home could be in a thousand places."

"Let's start looking," said Uncle Pete. He began to move off through the snow.

"That will take too long," said Cousin Dinky. "If Mother is in danger, she needs our help *now*."

"We can smoke them out," said Uncle Pete, "if we stop up this chimney."

"Good idea!" said Cousin Dinky. He grabbed a handful of snow.

"No," said Stubby Speck. He held Cousin Dinky's arm. "That won't work. They'll just put the fire out. They'll know we're here and come out and attack us."

"Let them!" said Uncle Pete. "If they come out, we'll find out where the entrance is. Then we can rush in and rescue Lily."

"It's too much of a risk," said Stubby Speck. "We have to do something that will make them come out so fast they won't have time to plan an attack."

"Yes, but what?" said Cousin Dinky. "We have to hurry."

"I hate to use this on anyone," said Stubby Speck. He patted a seed that was tied to his belt like a canteen. "But I'm afraid we'll have to."

"What is it?" said Cousin Dinky.

"This hollow seed has the worst-smelling stuff in the world in it," said Mr. Speck.

"Do you mean . . . ?" Mr. Little looked at the skunk.

"Right!" said Stubby Speck. "It's full of old Skunk's smelly stuff. We can drop it down the chimney."

"Phew!" said Tom. "A stink bomb!"

"My mother may be down there," said Cousin Dinky.

"It won't hurt anyone," said Stubby Speck. "It will only surprise them. They'll come out in a hurry, believe me."

"We don't even know if Aunt Lily is down there," said Mr. Little. "We don't even know if they are enemies."

"And we don't know if they are *not* enemies," said Uncle Pete. "They may have captured Lily. If they have, Speck's plan is a good one. Besides—it won't hurt them. It will only make them come out in a hurry. They'll walk right into our arms."

"Let's do *something!*" said Cousin Dinky. "Anything. Mother landed here, that's for sure. And if the Ground Tinies did capture her—what, oh what, have they done to her?"

Chapter Eleven

fter Aunt Lily was stuffed into the bag, she felt herself being picked up and carried. It was pitch black inside the bag. Aunt Lily tried to think. Right then she decided, no matter what happened, she would not scream again. She would try to be brave. After a while, she was set down on the ground.

"Make sure the bag be tightly tied, boys," said the husky-voiced man who had spoken before.

Someone's hands felt around the bag near Aunt Lily's ankles.

"Whatever are we going to do with it, Whit?" said a woman.

"I'm afraid to let it out," said Whit. He was the husky-voiced man.

"We need a weapon," said a young man.

"There'll be no weapons in this burrow," said the man called Whit. "We Snippets have never used weapons, and we never will. It's not our way. You know that, boy."

Aunt Lily sighed. "Thank the stars," she said aloud. "These are gentle people."

"Did you hear that, Whit Snippet?" said the woman. "You've got a woman in that bag there."

"You in the bag!" said Whit Snippet. "What do you Tree Tinies want in our part of the woods?"

"I'm not a Tree Tiny," said Aunt Lily. "I'm Lily Little. I live in the house of Dr. Dan Zigger."

Silence.

"Come now, miss," said Mr. Snippet. "No Tinies live in houses. It be well known."

"It's the truth," said Aunt Lily. "Tiny people live in houses all over the Big Valley."

"Don't trust her, Papa." It was another young man's voice. "It be a kind of Tree Tiny trick."

"Where be the Big Valley, miss?" said the woman.

"Hush, wife," said Whit Snippet. "*I'll* ask the questions." He cleared his throat. "Well, where *be* the Big Valley, miss?"

"Don't you think we could talk better if you let me out of this bag, Mr. Snippet?" said Aunt Lily.

"Don't trust her, Papa!" said one of the young men.

"She doesn't *sound* like a terrible person, Whit," said the woman.

"Will you please be quiet, wife? I'll handle this," said Whit Snippet. "Your mother is right, boys. She doesn't sound terrible."

"I still don't trust her," said the young man.

"Remember how she screamed when we captured her?" said the other.

"I was scared!" said Aunt Lily from the bag.

"*I* be the father here," said Whit Snippet. "And I say she doesn't sound terrible. Open the bag."

Chapter Twelve

unt Lily climbed out of the bag. She came face to face with the Whit Snippet family.

The Snippets were tiny people who lived under the ground in a rabbit burrow. Their underground home began where the rabbits' hole ended. There was a door separating the Snippets' rooms from the rabbits' nest.

The Snippets and the rabbits got along well together. The Snippets were timid —just like the rabbits. They would run away if strangers came near.

The entrance to the rabbit burrow was under the thornbush where Aunt Lily had landed in her parachute. The Snippets' rooms were deep in the ground under a large maple tree. The rooms were dug in among the roots of the maple tree.

The Snippets were tree-root benders. They could turn a tree root into a chair by whittling and carefully bending the growing root. The Snippets' rooms were full of tables, chairs, beds, cupboards, and desks. The Snippets had made all the furniture out of the roots of the maple tree.

There was a fireplace in each room. The fireplaces were needed to dry out the damp rooms. The chimneys for the fires came out of the ground in different places under the thornbush. The Snippets were experts at making fires that gave little smoke, and it was hard for anyone to spot a Snippet chimney from the outside.

THE · SNIPPET · FAMILY

"You don't look like you be a Tree Tiny," said Whit Snippet when Aunt Lily climbed out of the bag.

Aunt Lily blinked. The bright light from the beeswax candles hurt her eyes. She looked around the room at the Snippets.

Whit Snippet stood over her a full two inches. He was taller than Mr. Little, and thin. He had a little beard on his chin.

"She may be a Tree Tiny dressed up to fool us," said the taller Snippet son. He was even taller and thinner than his father.

"This is my nurse's uniform," said Aunt Lily. "I told you I wasn't a Tree Tiny."

"What were you doing throwing snow down my chimney?" said Whit Snippet.

"That was an accident," said Aunt Lily. She smiled. "I know it sounds silly, but I . . . I fell on your chimney when I landed in my parachute."

The Snippets looked at each other in surprise.

"You came out of the sky?" said Mr. Snippet.

"Tiny people don't fly," said the second son, who was younger and shorter than his brother.

"Some tiny people *do* fly indeed," said Aunt Lily. "My son is one of them. I fell out of his glider when it tipped over in the storm."

"We know nothing of this flying," said Mr. Snippet. "This be true?"

"You spoke of the Big Valley, miss," said Mrs. Snippet in the shadow behind her husband. "Where be this Big Valley?"

"I can see I've got a lot to explain," said Aunt Lily. "Can we sit down and talk?"

* * *

Aunt Lily knew she had to ask the Snippets for help. She knew she couldn't get to the Biggs' house alone. She didn't even know the right direction.

But Aunt Lily could see that the Snippets were afraid of her. She knew she would have to make them like her and trust her before they would want to help.

It was morning before Aunt Lily had answered most of the Snippets' questions. She learned much about them, too. She found that they were shy people who lived quietly in the woods. They didn't trust strangers, and they knew little about the world outside of their burrow.

They had seen tiny people living in trees, and they were afraid of them. The tree people carried weapons and always ran after the Snippets when they saw them.

The Snippets never dreamed that some tiny people were brave enough to live in the houses of the big people. If a big person got anywhere near their underground home, they ran to the deepest room in the burrow until he passed. Then they would talk about it for days afterward, as though it had been an earthquake.

Aunt Lily found out there were other underground people like the Snippets. "Where are they?" said Aunt Lily. "I'd like to meet more underground people."

Whit Snippet answered, "It not be Meeting Day. They won't come if it not be Meeting Day."

The Snippets told Aunt Lily that the underground people met once a month on Meeting Day in a great hall. Sometimes they came to each other's burrows, but mostly they liked to meet in the great hall. The hall was deeper in the earth than any of their homes, and it was a very secret place. On Meeting Day the underground people talked, danced and played games from early morning until late at night.

While Mr. Snippet was telling Aunt Lily about Meeting Day, Mrs. Snippet cooked breakfast. She hurried in and out of the room so she would not miss any of the talk.

Aunt Lily had breakfast with her new friends. They ate hot wild oatmeal. The oatmeal was spiced with home-dried raisins and sweetened with wild bees' honey.

Finally, when the Snippets seemed more friendly toward her, Aunt Lily said, "Do you like babies, Mr. Snippet?"

"I do like babies," said the tall thin man. "Mrs. Snippet always wanted a girl baby after we had our two boys, but we never had one."

Mrs. Snippet nodded.

"It's very important that I leave you soon," said Aunt Lily, "to help the Littles. They're going to have a new baby."

"Be they the folks you were flying to see?" said Mr. Snippet.

"Yes," said Aunt Lily. "Mrs. Little is going to have a baby, and she needs me. Will you please help me get there?"

Whit Snippet got up from his seat and walked back and forth. "We never leave the woods, Miss Lily," he said. "It be a bad thing to do."

"It be too far to go," said the older son.

"We be caught by Tree Tinies," said the younger son. "And Miss Lily, we all be *killed*."

"Miss Lily says the mother needs her," said Mrs. Snippet. "I think we should help."

"Hush, woman!" said Mr. Snippet. "You wash the dishes. *I* decide the thing."

Chapter Thirteen

ey!" said Tom Little. "I can hear *voices* in the chimney."

Cousin Dinky rushed to the Snippets' chimney. He put his ear close to the opening.

"What do you hear?" said Uncle Pete.

"Shhh! Listen!" said Cousin Dinky. He put his finger up to his lips.

The others crowded around the chimney. Aunt Lily was speaking. They could only hear a few words. Aunt Lily was asking the Snippets to help her get to the Littles. But the tiny men outside heard just the words "... please help me ..."

"It's Lily!" said Uncle Pete. "She needs help. Don't just stand there."

"Shhh, Uncle Pete," said Mr. Little. "We can't hear."

By this time Whit Snippet's younger son was telling Aunt Lily they might all be killed by Tree Tinies if they helped her. This is what came out of the chimney: "... Tree Tinies ... Miss Lily ... be *killed*."

"Great Scott!" said Uncle Pete. "The brutes are going to *kill* her!"

Cousin Dinky grabbed the firecracker Tom had brought with him. "We've got to stop them," he yelled. He got out his match and lighted the fuse. "Where's the stink bomb?"

Stubby Speck handed the seed to Cousin Dinky.

Cousin Dinky dropped the firecracker and the seed down the chimney at the same time.

"Do you think that was wise, Dinky?" said Mr. Little. "Your mother is down there."

"We've got to stop them," said Cousin Dinky. "You heard what he said. They are going to kill her!"

BANG! The firecracker went off inside the Snippets' fireplace.

"Watch for them to come out!" yelled Mr. Speck.

"Phew!" said Uncle Pete. "Let's get away from this chimney."

A few second later Tom saw the Snippets and Aunt Lily. "There they are! They're escaping on rabbits!"

"There's Lily!" shouted Uncle Pete.

"She's tied to a rabbit!"

The rabbits ran off into the underbrush.

"Get aboard Skunk!" yelled Stubby Speck. "We'll track them down."

The tiny people struggled through the deep snow to where the skunk was standing. Everybody climbed on.

"Get moving, Skunk!" yelled Mr. Speck.

The skunk waddled slowly off after the rabbits.

Cousin Dinky pounded his hand with his fist. "It's no use," he said. "This skunk will never catch them."

"They have to stop sometime," said Stubby Speck. "We'll follow their tracks until they do."

"They're probably taking Aunt Lily to another hide-out," said Uncle Pete, "now that we've found this one."

* * *

Nobody was more surprised than the Littles and Stubby Speck when the rabbit tracks led them to . . . the Biggs' house!

Of course, they were a long time getting there. The skunk, true to his nature, never went faster than skunks are supposed to go.

"I don't understand," said Mr. Little. "What do you think they are doing here?"

"*I* understand," said Uncle Pete. "The Ground Tinies made Aunt Lily tell where she was going. They came to attack our family while we were away."

"Is that possible?" said Mr. Little. "Would Aunt Lily . . . ?"

"They probably thought the menfolk would be out looking for your Aunt Lily," said Stubby Speck.

"Aunt Lily would never tell," said Tom.

"They tricked her into telling," said Uncle Pete.

"Let's get in there," said Cousin Dinky. He leaped off the skunk as soon as he got close to the house.

The tiny people entered the Biggs' house through a secret door known only to the Littles.

"We've got them trapped," said Uncle Pete. He was running and waving his sword. "We'll make them pay if they've done anything."

Mr. Little was worried now. He threw open the door to the Littles' rooms. They all rushed in, weapons ready.

No one.

"Search the other rooms!" yelled Uncle Pete. "Hurry!"

The five tiny people ran from room to room. At last Mr. Little opened the door to his bedroom.

Mrs. Little was lying in bed holding a sleeping baby in her arms. Aunt Lily, Granny Little, Lucy Little, Mr. and Mrs. Whit Snippet and their two sons were standing near her. Everyone was smiling.

Aunt Lily put her finger to her lips. "Shhh!" she said. "Keep those men quiet, Will, or they'll wake up your new baby."

"But," said Mr. Little. "We thought..."

"Will," said Mrs. Little, "I'd like you to meet Mr. and Mrs. Whit Snippet and their two sons. If it weren't for these brave people, Aunt Lily never would have gotten here in time to welcome Betsy Little into the world."

"Wow!" said Tom Little. "She's a girl!"

Lucy Little laughed. "Come here, Tom, and look at her," she said. "She's so *tiny!*"